For Tara and Alexandra   KH

To Mary Craig, with love   HC

PUFFIN BOOKS

Published by the Penguin Group
Penguin Books Ltd, 80 Strand, London WC2R 0RL, England
Penguin Putnam Inc., 375 Hudson Street, New York, New York 10014, USA
Penguin Books Australia Ltd, 250 Camberwell Road, Camberwell, Victoria 3124, Australia
Penguin Books Canada Ltd, 10 Alcorn Avenue, Toronto, Ontario, Canada M4V 3B2
Penguin Books India (P) Ltd, 11 Community Centre, Panchsheel Park, New Delhi – 110 017, India
Penguin Books (NZ) Ltd, Cnr Rosedale and Airborne Roads, Albany, Auckland, New Zealand
Penguin Books (South Africa) (Pty) Ltd, 24 Sturdee Avenue, Rosebank 2196, South Africa

Penguin Books Ltd, Registered Offices: 80 Strand, London WC2R 0RL, England

www.penguin.com

First published by Aurum Press Ltd 1984
Published by Viking 2001
5 7 9 10 8 6 4
Published in Puffin Books 2001
9 10 8

Copyright © HIT Entertainment plc, 2001
Text copyright © Katharine Holabird, 1984
Illustrations copyright © Helen Craig Ltd, 1984

Angelina, Angelina Ballerina and the Dancing Angelina logo are trademarks of HIT Entertainment plc,
Katharine Holabird and Helen Craig Ltd. Angelina is registered in the UK, Japan and US Pat. & Tm. Off.
The Dancing Angelina logo is registered in the UK.

Manufactured in China by South China Printing Ltd. Co.

British Library Cataloguing in Publication Data
A CIP catalogue record for this book is available from the British Library

ISBN 0–670–91153–4 Hardback
ISBN 0–140–56862–X Paperback

To find out more about Angelina, visit her web site at **www.angelinaballerina.com**

Angelina
and the Princess

Story by Katharine Holabird Illustrations by Helen Craig

PUFFIN

Angelina was much too excited to sleep. The students at Miss Lilly's Ballet School had been asked to dance for Her Royal Highness, the Princess of Mouseland. Mr Lightfoot, Director of the famous Royal Ballet Company, was coming tomorrow to help Miss Lilly choose the best ballerinas for the special performance. Angelina wanted a leading part so much that she worked on her pliés and pirouettes far into the night when she should have been sound asleep.

The next morning Angelina woke up feeling terrible. Her head ached and her ears buzzed. Angelina's mother took her temperature and shook her head sadly. "I'm afraid you'll have to stay in bed," she said. "You can't go to ballet school when you're not well."

But Angelina was determined to go. While her mother was busy downstairs Angelina packed her ballet bag …

… and tiptoed out of the house.

Angelina arrived at Miss Lilly's Ballet School just in time to join her friends Flora and Felicity and all the other ballerinas who were waiting to go on stage. Flora did a nimble leap and a delicate spin …

… and then it was Angelina's turn to dance. Her heart started beating like a drum and she couldn't remember what she was supposed to be doing.

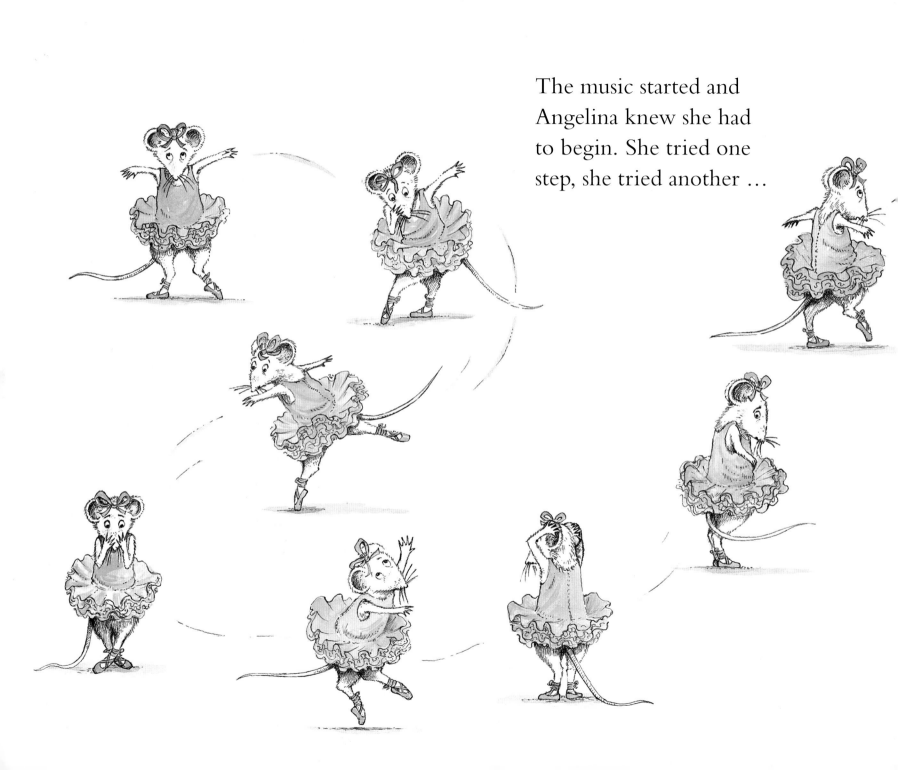

The music started and Angelina knew she had to begin. She tried one step, she tried another …

… then she began twirling and spinning like a top until she was so dizzy she lost her balance, tripped on her pink ribbons and tumbled down with a thump.

Flora and Felicity were given the leading roles in the
Dance of the Flower Fairies. Later, Miss Lilly called for
Angelina. "I'm afraid you will have to take a smaller
part this time," she said, trying to be kind.

When Angelina got home her mother was very upset.
"How could you run away like that when I told you to
stay in bed?" she asked.

Angelina burst into tears. "I had to go to Miss Lilly's, but everything went wrong. I danced so badly for Mr Lightfoot, I will never be a real ballerina. I am not going to ballet school any more."

Angelina's mother hugged her and kissed her and
carried her upstairs, and in just a minute she was
fast asleep in her own bed again.

The next day Angelina's headache was gone.
She felt better, but she was still very sad.
"It's not fair!" said Angelina.

"Maybe not," her mother said gently, "but things don't always go our way. You can still do your best with whatever part you are given, and that will help the whole performance."

Angelina thought about what her mother had said. Then she returned to Miss Lilly's after all, and rehearsed very hard with the other ballerinas for the Royal Performance.

After she had learned her own part, she memorized
the Dance of the Flower Fairies while watching
Flora and Felicity.

On the day of the Royal Performance, just as the show
was about to begin, Flora tripped and sprained her ankle.
Everyone was terribly upset.

Mr Lightfoot and Miss Lilly turned to each other in
horror. "Who can do the part?" they cried. Angelina
was worried about Flora, but Susie stepped forward
and said, "Angelina can!"

Angelina showed Miss Lilly that she had learned the dance by heart. "But what about Flora?" she asked.

"Don't worry," said Miss Lilly, "we have a treat for her …"

… So Flora was happy because she was invited to sit right next to the Princess of Mouseland. Mr Lightfoot and Miss Lilly were happy because the performance could go on. Angelina was happy because she did the Dance of the Flower Fairies without forgetting a single step. The Princess of Mouseland was happy because she loved ballet.

When the performance was over she congratulated Angelina
and thanked her warmly for saving the show.